FAIR PLAY

BY GINA AND MERCER MAYER

Originally published in a different format by Reader's Digest.

www.littlecritter.com

Printed in China
46763201 2014

Published by FastPencil PREMIERE
307 Orchard City Drive, Suite 210, Campbell CA 95008
Premiere.FastPencil.com

THAT'S NOT FAIR

BY GINA AND MERCER MAYER

Sometimes things just aren't fair.

I had to make my bed. That wasn't fair.
It was just going to get messed up again.

I wanted to give my sister a haircut,
but Mom said, "No, you can't."
That wasn't fair.

So I gave my sister's doll
a haircut instead.

I wanted to eat watermelon in the living room, but my Mom made me go back in the kitchen. That wasn't fair.

We went to the mall to get me some new clothes. I didn't want new clothes.

I wanted to go to the toy store,
but Mom said, "Not now."

I had to try on a pair of pants
and a sweater.

I wanted to get an ice cream cone, but Mom said, “We don’t have time.”

So I asked to go to the candy store instead. We couldn’t do that either.

I didn’t get to do anything I wanted to do. It just wasn’t fair.

On the way home, I turned on my ray gun. Dad made me stop because the baby was sleeping.
I said, "That's not fair."
Dad said, "Things aren't always fair."

Later, when I made a tent out of
Mom's bedspread, Mom said,
"You have a tent outside."

I said, "I don't want to play outside."
I had to go out anyway. Was that fair?

I found a skunk in the garden. I wanted to bring him in the house to feed him, but Mom and Dad screamed, "No!" That wasn't fair. The skunk was really hungry.

I wanted to take my brother for
a bike ride, but Mom said he
was too little.
He wanted to go. It wasn’t fair.

Later Dad made me give the dog
a bath. That wasn't fair. My dog
likes to be dirty.

At dinner I ate all my carrots, but
I had to take out the trash anyway.
I knew that wasn't fair.

Then I had to take a bath. That wasn't fair. I like to be dirty, too.

CRITTER NEWS

When I wanted to finger-paint, Dad
said, "Not now—you've just had a bath."
I got mad. I yelled, "That's not fair!"
Dad made me go to my room
until I said I was sorry.

I said I was sorry even though it wasn't fair. I just wanted to watch TV.

Mom and Dad say that sometimes things
just aren't fair. But there is one thing
that I know is fair…

I get to stay up later than my sister and brother every single night.

I DIDN'T KNOW THAT

BY GINA AND MERCER MAYER

There are lots of things that I don't know.
I didn't know that if I ate a whole bag
of candy, my tummy would hurt.

I didn't know that if I left my bear out in the rain, it would get ruined. I thought it would get clean.

I didn't know that if I left my crayons on the floor,
my baby brother would write on the walls.

I didn't know that if I left the top off the box, my snake would crawl out.

I also didn't know that my mom
was so scared of snakes.

I didn't know that if I left the freezer door open, all the ice cream would melt. But I did know that I wasn't supposed to leave the freezer door open.

1 2 3 4 5
6 7 8 9 10 11 12
13 14 15
20 21
27

I knew that I wasn't supposed to push my sister too high on the swing. I just forgot.

I didn't know that if I pulled my cat's tail, she would scratch me. I thought she liked to play.

I didn't know that I wasn't supposed
to play with Dad's shaving cream.
I was just pretending.

I didn't know that blowing soda bubbles
through my straw would make
such a big mess.

I didn't know that I had to put away everything I took out. If I had known that, I would have been more careful.

I didn't know that "please" was a magic word.
PLEASE?

I didn't know that my brother was too little to play monsters. I think he makes a good monster.

I didn’t know that flying a kite
near trees isn’t a good idea.

I didn’t know that eating spinach
would give me big muscles.
But I still don’t like spinach.

I didn't know that Dad and Mom hadn't
read the newspaper yet.
The dog didn't know it either.

CRITTER DAILY

I didn't know that my cat wasn't allowed to sleep on my bed. Well, maybe I did know that.

There are all kinds of things that I don't know.

I guess that's why there are grown-ups.

JUST A LITTLE DIFFERENT

BY GINA AND MERCER MAYER

BIJOUX
SILENT
MOVERS

A new critter moved into a house in my neighborhood. His name is Zack. His family is just a little different than the rest of the families on our block, because his father is a turtle and his mother is a rabbit.

My family and I went to visit Zack and his family. They were very friendly, but Zack was a little shy.

Later at baseball practice, I said to the critters,
"Let's ask Zack to join our team."

But the other critters didn't want to.
One of them said, "He's just too different to be on our team."

That made me mad. I told Mom and Dad
Mom said, "Being different is good. Our
differences make us special."

I decided Zack wasn't too different to be my friend. I went over to ask him to come and play at my house. His mom said he could.

Playing with Zack was fun. We made some big buildings. Then we made ourselves into big monsters who could knock the buildings down.

When I went to Zack's house, he showed me his computer. We drew some cool pictures on it for our moms.

Zack and I liked playing the same things. We played video games.

We played hide-and-seek from my sister.

We rode our bikes.

We even played cowboys.
I told my friends that Zack was a lot of fun.

But they still thought he was just too different. One of the critters made fun of Zack. That really made me mad.

One day Zack and I decided to build a clubhouse. We got some scraps of wood and some tools.
Zack's dad helped us.

While we were working, some of the critters walked by.
"What are you doing?" they asked.
We told them.

They thought it was so cool they wanted
to join our club, too.
Zack said they could.

We worked on the clubhouse all day. We all had fun together.

When the clubhouse was finished, we had our first club meeting. We decided that Zack should be club leader, since the clubhouse was in his yard.

And the other critters asked Zack to be on
our baseball team.
He plays first base.

Now Zack is one of the gang.
It doesn't matter to anyone that he's just a little different. He's the most popular crtiter in the neighborhood.

But I'm still his best friend.

THE SCHOOL PLAY

BY GINA AND MERCER MAYER

Class Play
Ou
Fc
Fri
Our Forest Friends

My teacher said, “We’re going to put on a school play, and all your families will be invited.” I thought that sounded cool.

My teacher gave us our parts. I was supposed to say, "Welcome to our forest. The trees are happy to see you."

When I got home I told Mom and Dad about the play. They said they couldn't wait to see it.

Mom made my costume. I was a green elf.
I felt sort of silly. At least I didn't
have to be a sunflower.

I practiced my lines for the play every day.
I practiced in the bathtub.

I practiced for my
baby brother.

I practiced for
my sister.

I even practiced for my dog.
He got my paper and chewed it up.

At school we practiced our parts when we were supposed to be having math. That was neat.

When the night of the play came, I put on my costume. We all went to school—even my baby brother. Mom promised to keep him quiet so he wouldn't ruin the play.

My family sat in the audience. I got to go up onstage. I felt so important. Then, while the principal was talking, I looked out from behind the curtain. I didn't know so many people were coming.

PRINCIPAL

My tummy started hurting. My teacher said it was just a little case of stage fright.

But when the curtain came up and the play started, my tummy didn't stop hurting.

First the sunflower said his part really loud, just the way the teacher told us.

Then it was my turn.

The audience was very quiet.
Everyone was waiting for me
to say my part. I was so scared,
I couldn't remember what to say.

Then I heard my baby brother in the audience saying, "Crido, Crido." That's what he calls me.

And everyone laughed. Then I remembered my part and I said it really loud.

I felt proud because I did a good job.
No one ever knew I almost forgot.

Now that the school play is over, I guess it wasn't so bad. I don't think I'll be so scared next time.

I'll just have to make sure my baby brother
sits in the front row!